This book belongs to:

First published in 2014 by Hodder Children's Books
This paperback edition first published in 2015

Text copyright © Peter Bently 2014
Illustration copyright © Sarah Massini 2014

Hodder Children's Books
338 Euston Road, London NW1 3BH

Hodder Children's Books Australia
Level 17/207 Kent Street, Sydney, NSW 2000

A catalogue record of this book is available from the British Library.

ISBN: 978 1 444 91377 4
10 9 8 7 6 5 4 3 2 1

Printed in China

Hodder Children's Books is a division of Hachette Children's Books.
An Hachette UK Company

www.hachette.co.uk

For Trudy and Tira, the mum and baby who gave me the idea - P.B.
For Alexander, sprinkled with love - S.M.

A Recipe for Bedtime

Peter Bently
& Sarah Massini

Hodder
Children's
Books

A division of Hachette Children's Books

Baby, baby soft and sweet,
Almost good enough to eat!

It's night-night time so come with me,
And hear my bedtime recipe.

Take a bundle full of joy
(It can be either girl or boy).

Snuggle in your arms, like so.

Unwrap gently,

top...

...to toe.

Check those tootsies,
Can you see

the little piggy?
Wee-
wee-
wee!

Add to water (not too hot).

Stir a little. Then a lot.

Scoop up baby. Place on mat.

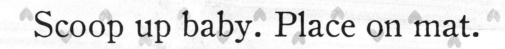

Dab the drips off, pat, pat, pat.

Where's that baby?

Peek - a - BOO!

Add raspberries to tummy, too.
It should be warm and soft as silk.

Wrap once more.

And then add milk.

Put in warm place. Cover tightly.
Add some kisses. Sprinkle lightly.

Leave to settle
for the night.

Sneak out softly.
Switch off the light.

Check on baby now and then.
If required, add milk again.

It often helps the job along
If you sing a little song –

Hush-a-bye fingers, hush-a-bye toes,
Hush-a-bye lips and hush-a-bye nose.
The Dream Fairy's coming to bring you sweet dreams
Down from the moon on silvery beams.
Hush-a-bye, hush-a-bye, close your eyes tight.

Night-night, my darling.
My darling, night-night.

Other great Hodder picture books to share with children:

Is it bedtime Wibbly Pig?
Mick Inkpen

The Cat, the Mouse and the Runaway Train
PETER BENTLY & STEVE COX

GOOD KNIGHT SLEEP TIGHT
DAVID MELLING

WHO Woke the Animals?
CHARLES FUGE AND DAVID CONWAY

THE TOOTH FAIRY'S CHRISTMAS
PETER BENTLY · GARRY PARSONS